T0120917

Other books by Mr. Rodney Paul Banks

Even Shorter Stories I

Even Shorter Stories II

RODNEY PAUL WILLIAMS

authorHOUSE®

AuthorHouse™
1663 Liberty Drive
Bloomington, IN 47403
www.authorhouse.com
Phone: 833-262-8899

Published by AuthorHouse 07/13/2022

ISBN: 978-1-6655-6503-5 (sc)
ISBN: 978-1-6655-6502-8 (e)

CONTENTS

LIVING

When I give my word I keep my word, so here is Even Shorter Stories II.
If you posses the book then please read even shorter stories first or it will
be missing the stand of a quadrilogy. I want to promise you readers four
books in order yet my talent my no stretch that far. Lu, my best.

Prelude to War of the Worlds

The meeting took place in front of billions of pairs of eyes and yet it was kept to secret for chief executives only. Eleven of the most popular major players attended. P from nineteen oh eight. CP from eighteen seventy five. M from Seventeen fifty seven. M from nineteen thirty four. S from nineteen oh five. T from eighteen eighty. S.P oversaw and chaired and was the oldest to attend C from eighteen fifty four asked all to attend. C from the second oldest of the attendees, second only to C from eighteen fifty four. L from eighteen seventy three and lastly and the youngest to attend, L from nineteen oh six. All answered eye at roll call.

This meeting is held for one purpose and one purpose only announced chair small pot, the annihilation of all human kind. Eleven have answered and are present. How say you, yes or only on the subject? From order of your assigned number please vote. Each in form voted in the affirmative the chair voting lost made the vote unanimous.

L, being the youngest of those asked to attend was allows to read the charges against mankind.

Every since our existence, each of us at separate times, when man discovered we were alive and sentient may lies determined to destroy us. Every other form created by Jealous has let us be only mankind has invalidated of right to coexist. Man has denied all eleven of us and everyone of our brethren kind life. This ends the report of the changes. These changes have been on this date read to you by your extended family member Choler. Therefore my duty being consummate Cholera yields the floor.

IMPORTED

Because of the game lost Osanii Rojes right field for the New York Mets made his bid to have the best throwing 31m in major league baseball last night.

All of the sports world is talking about the throw he made from the corner of the right to first base.

Runners were on first and second in the first innings. Tejark Redneck batting four in Tigers line up gave a crack of forty ounce. The ball out of the park over the right field wall. Osanii leaped for it. His base hand over the fence caught it. The runners believing it was gone had taken off.

Matt Jefefsuss was on second had almost made it to home plate when he headed to third on his way back to second base. Smitty White about to tog third went back to first. Smitty unlike Matt ran directly to first base running over the pitcher's mound. Shortest distant between two points. He was still out. The togging of first base was so quick due Osanii's powerful arm that Matt was tripled up at second base. The Mets went on twin the game one-zero.

Rojas is a rookie starter here from the Cuban baseball league. The rookie is on the road to greatness. Had he let the ball just to outside side of the foul line instead of bustling to change the course of the game. Redneck might not have been shaken up just enough to throw his concentration off. Redneck is a serious high percentage batting average. Last year he batted three twenty with fifty diggers.

On Stage Skit S.K.S.

Hey! Cos. You didn't think of this one.

Thought I would let you know why the war of the worlds did not happen. Before continuing thought I feel it only fair. I explain these couple of facts. First off there may be a possibility that Martians do not exist. If they do not exist there is no Martian language. Second any most profound of the two if Martians do exist the probability is if they do not speak the American language then there is truth that I won't be able to understand it. My bad. If there is no earthly language on Mars you won't understand their word either. So there! Think you smarter than are hunk.

I decided Mars and Martians do cohabit in this solar system and since you cannot comprehend Martian I will put this is the language of the U.S. of A. Yeah.

The first clue I took notice of where the blue jets of flame. Blue flames from a red planet. The fust thing coming to my mind were Republicans and Democrats.

So they finally were at war as did the U.S.A. you know the one. The confederate Democrats verging the Union Republicans.

No, No, I wasn't around at that time to report the truth on that one.

Ok, so the wealthy Martians revolt and attack the poor Martian ruled government.

The poor had to be overthrown. Most of the poor were petty thieves, subsisting on welfare to damned lazy to go to college which would order there lowliness ended. Most were truly slovenly. Dropping empty containers and trash on the public walkways. Some you could see they did not keep their own homes by entuents, or rented rooms clean. You could observe that even if you didn't even know them or where their abode was made for them during the warm spring seasons and the summers wee they were sandals or flip-flops. You could see the bottoms of their feet were really @ thily cruddy. They'd leave there refuse on the public riding conveyances.

The wealthy become loathsome towards them continuing to dole out funds so could have a dwelling, food, clothing and utilities when all that was needed to become self sufficient was schooling to get a good paying societal helpful meets of employment. I had now been six decades of this uneasiness, thus the explosions of blue flame.

You may believe the wealthy was bombing the poor on a major Kvel. Not sooo

They poor learned to attack themselves trying to attain or attaining in some cases the little comforts or impoverished had. Underline the word had. They had none left to pay their way.

The wealthy disguised their abandonment of the undesirables as going on vacation via privately space ship companies. What really happened, they moved to . . earth.

There wealth of goods as their wealth of knowledge, accepted.

DETECTIVE MAN IN THE CASE OF,

THE HOLLOW TUSK

THE HOLLOW TUSK

Dedicated to, Misses Leona Demaris Banks, the woman, JEALOUS, loomed me to be my mother and bring me to HIM.

CHAPTER ONE

ELATEDNESS ABANDON

"It is all but over now." Overheard by a sole bystander. Cascades of barely expressionless college of black, brown, Caucasian and yellow faces - yellow including Asian and Latino the second and the third most populace races in that order in here U.S.PA.

CHAPTER TWO

IT LOOKS GOOD

The meeting ended with Saki Havored with green ginger other tumbler led to vast amounts of huge and hearty batches, some piggishly expelling bits of warm Brother's from clear glass under gallon barrels. Brothers over the past two centuries had become the brandy of the utmost elites rulers on Earth.

New decided and having agreed unanimously on low income hogging for all citizens of Nigeria. Angela, Congo, Libya, Nigeria and Sudan.

The agreed dictators transcribed and delivered to each countries housing's chief administrator by hand. Strictly for security purposes.

Those who were receivers of the edicts had been legally mandated to take the dictates into actuality were made reticent by armed guards insuring recieval to their own country's dictator.

In the country of China, Beijing, Talmud Quran banks, opened his eyes. Speculation, he would singularly but barely have an ability to view only the lights above. The one absolute the medium, bumby sized, brown nipple, allowed directly between lips gave exhaustive relief. Momentarily her happiness glowed the opense of her lips, he is contentedly sucking. As though he knew the supply we can only guess would not succumb to emptiness.

That being expressed all that needs be elucidated odely necessary to be reported this Talmud Quran banks is supposed to be destined to the heights of praisable glory. The only offspring of Yendor Luap Banks who when but in his fourteenth year of life did disarm & corrupt cop from Briffbay town Novascocia, while pointing the semi-automatic handgun at his now prey never took his eyes from his biological parents would be murderer. You're not going to shoot the safety is still on. Talmud had quickly removed the weapon from the cop's holster. About to seize the moment the cop was sadly dismayed as Talmud angled the automatic slightly to the ground, staring directly coldly into his soon to be dead opponents, released the safety stepped one long step backwards raised the weapon and emptied the eight shot chip into the throat privates and then the head. "The safety's off now he finally allowed from his quiet lips."

The safety thumbed off as Talmud took one large backward, thinking to himself the child's game may I.

The spots on the ground grew together into one large pool. Life oozed together as breathing desisted, and awareness hitted, the clip now seven cartridges lighter.

THE PRICE OF OVERNIGHT FORTUNE AND FAME

A couple of his inventions were the human washing machine. It cleansed the entire human body, removing: glues, inks, urine, fecesi oleo and natural body grime. Another was truly inventive, needed and saved lives. The apparatus he sold attached to automobile bottoms in winter like regions. The heat from the engines were expelled from attached stainless steel tubes into ice and snow making roads unslippery. Saving salting asphalt thus maintaining maintenance free highways and city streets by omitting the damage done by saltings.

A deca billionaire thirty times over almost overnight. Every auto in every developed country mandatorily by how come equipped with the Banks Bar.

Photographed on magazines covering this planet, not a major television night show host and no top anchorman missed him for interviews. Major leaders of all the civilized first world countries had invited him to their homes for dinner. Most citizen the ruler's most expensive alcoholic beverage was offered and he a tea totaler. His disappearance could not go un-noticed.

GIRRRRRRRR......

Something within brain. I want to wake up! I want to wake up! As I begin recognize the painful plea, simultaneously, I want to wake up! The agonizing loudness though just as concerned has conceived my acceptance its presence quiets to a deafening roar. Neither my conscious nor my subconscious has maintained copies receptive cognition.

What disturbs mostly is now my education I had been receiving would assist me in tonight's upcoming discussion on Friday's coming classroom debate. My attentiveness interruption has sporadically diluted to almost knowing zonk.

Inwardly where it belongs my fear, my sorrow has solved itself into anger. Anger with my own brain. This disappointment in my fatherhood indubitably apprised my subconscious to shut the fuck up!!!

Having gotten back on track. Ordered the rescheduling of that program on pay-per-view with my assistance & perfectly done was on her grading paper Monday morning.

My loved one being best in class awarded her mom, two sibs and me to a full four course expensive dinner with desserts Saturday night. The check only cost me twenty one hundred dollars.

Her doctorate in terraforming life skills has lender her third position on the NASA first landing on the first habitat planet outside this Milky Way galaxy.

SUCKERS

After the riots is when it will be time to cash in, those stupid slimey characterized people are going to make our profits for the next two fiscal quarters skyrocket.

For the minor pesky little bit of damages and their petty ass thievery our insurance companies will pay out of their assets. Their coffers will pay all the damages even the cost of labor to repair.

We will get paid for all the merchandise, both stolen and destroyed, Merchandise that could possible never have been sold. Who knows?

The coup da gras is when we do reopen for business the prices for everything we do sell will have been inflated by us and customers will pay. Without complaint!

The commercial should have conveyed, shoplifters and rioters takes everybody's money, except for the people you steal from.

THE GAVEL COMES DOWN

The strongest criminal case he had ever won was the case of the state of Tennessee US. Oakland Kerbaugh.

With the seemingly insignificant testimony of his client & not guilty verdict was celebrated with a full magnum of Syrah, a fine red wine.

Not guilty on all four charges of murder in the first degree.

The verdict had been the most important of all time. Kerbaugh admitted to his lawyer that he took the lives of all four women he had seriously dated and on married and was divorced from. This mediocre attorney when he had heard his client's confession immediately cholked this case another loss, then his client explained his motives.

Nine months and three days later.

Ordinarily I must confess for the confession from an accused that four murders was given of ones own will I would have thrown the book on top of him helping weigh down the hefty poundage of the prison he would most assuredly spend the remaining portion of one's entire life. Also I give myself congratulatory worm toddy of brandy and tea. Kissed my woman extensively goodnight and slept like an undisturbed child. During those proceedings I knew way of thinking opened my eyes and legally, legally mind you I know posses a new attitude.

Mister Lester your client has convinced me had he not taken the matter into his own hands then the lives of future unconceived offspring. Would not have been conceived. Therefore you may by my judgement tell your client to go home. My decision is not guilty. The gavel comes down.

Mouth to A

Usually do not hold back on facts when coming on your show. But since you asked the oddest case ever treated was told by a proctologist. Should have been by an orthodontist, during an anal examination she pulled out a dental whitening strip.

I can only imagine the possibilities. She is a small mouth model. She was making another to commercial for Dert strip. That is my best guess.

Another bite out of crime

From the clerks in every one of your facilities. Six months to be seen by a doctor. Six months for an appointment. No wonder you have had a few deaths.

First by firing all your appointment desk employees you save over fifty billion in operating cost by hiring new employees. You can pay lower wages to the newly hired staff. Fidd onto that the reason you dismiss your current employees can be acceptable in every court where Victor torch and the Prime minister were in a meeting when Marion Wayne was introduced.

Mister Torch, Prime minister, he greeted. Mister Wayne come an melodic chime.

Let us get right down to business. Only one thing can be ascertained. The two of you firing that Medical Chief Garth Zotaki was the worse move you could have done. All of hospitals have the same problem. That you were spot on. Even though Zotaki headed all of them he was not the problem. Your problem came you deny the deposed employees unemployment benefits. No pensions will be paid due to inefficient dismissal those employees who would retire. Lastly you get this advice. Follow the advice of the efficiently expert you hired. I charged you eleven and a half million.

Gentleman that is it. I have no more to report. Stay healthy and be erect. Good bye. He exits. The door closes, the two smile. Everything is as expected.

BRAIN

Finally in the upper class Melinda the three kids mother was easily calmed down from her almost reaching tiradical protest of the man I hired to sit her school ones. She comes to me to fire him complaining he allowed too much watching of that damned ole idiot box.

I showed what I found over a month prior. Their graded school test papers all had slight improvements. I also allowed to know what I had learned watching the six p.m. news with them that self same day. Cuba is in a closer proximity to the U.S. than in Puerto Rica.

Her smirk gave me reason to exclaim. My explanation was that programs be allowed to watch most frequently taught geography, safety being areas were drug was in the ghetto were occurring. Others were brought to view, such over the telephone and computer scams stealing from the beguiled.

Then as she thinking turned quieted and began the journey to her powder room, I went down the stairway and gave him his twenty four hour notice.

Melinda has such a great shape and walk. Nice little tusk. She has kept it clean. Even without her Law De Temp perfume, her own personal fragrance commands me. Even though I refuse to enter when she makes use of one of our lavatory to expel solid waste. I still know there is never embarrassment when the expurgates.

Memory Part 1

Twenty minutes to seven o' clock am the call to two one five g-e-t-a-a-b is made.

Seven o' clock a.m his cell phone chimes. I am outside Mister Gillette, announces the taxi cab driver. His reply as usual, is right down.

Recognizing the Ford Concord, all get A-Gab cars are unmarked with advertisement. This driver had picked him up about four years ago from the fifty bars. The day was continuing nicely with a pleasant memory. On that trip the driver kept his own eyes on traffic and the road to their destination mostly.

Good morning to the driver. Thank you, yes and a good morning to you to.

The destination given and a request for the cost of the fare were answered with thirty four fifteen. A fifty is passed of front along with a keep the change.

Smiles from both. The driver due to his large tip. The passenger because he recalls that that driver is a true professional. As he recalls his last ride with this cheefer like taxi handler was smoother than his pick up hire he had used on the exotic dancer he had in the taxi chiver's car the last time.

The auto put into gear never moved an inch towards its predetermined destination. A small truck sized meter crushed into the now crushed flaming used to be a vehicle.

Memory Part 2

Eight cases military concussion grenades fifteen crates A.R fifteens with four hundred cases ammo. Seventeen cases gas grenades. Eleven cases C.M seven military grade gas masks. Nineteen cases forty five automatics. Nine cases extra forty five automatic clips and lastly forty cases forty five automatic bullets.

They all check out boss. Give him his diamond hours, says the boss.

Hands are shook. Boooomm! is the sound juggady-juggady-juggadi-ve vecerrous is the sound accompanying the booommm! The quarter of an acre sized meteor that landed on the farms born where the illegal arms deal had only seconds prior been sealed.

There are no survivors save the truck delivery driver and the driver of the tractor trailer driver the arms were supposed to be landed on.

History could not record the day the Earth would have preferred to having stood still

The flying saucer from somewhere in the outer space lander in the vastness of a grassy parkland of Pendjari in Benin Africa.

The government having only hour or so indicating the unexpected and unprecedented sighting of the outer space craft's sudden hovering only fifty miles above the country. Only nominal military support had the time to answer the Oba Benin's sale leader. More were in the process trip of arrival.

The red colored craft was surrounded as the longigal walkway extended from the arrowhead shaped conveyance.

The occupant in gear allowing adfedtation to Earth's atmosphere calmly and slowly but with confidence progressed towards the crowd.

Tejag, the darmee of this Benmian quadrant along with his armed aid approached the arrival. Recognizing the approaching Earthing's the outerspace alien reached inside its mental capacity and in what should be recognized as a hand appeared a cylindrical shaped tiny but viewable silverish object and was allowing the advancing men to accept the gift. Misunderstanding this intention the aid gave warning to his superior not to worry his weapon won't be able to be used I am going to shoot. The Oba's order was barely asked of the shots fired.

The alien hit the grass and as the Oba and his aid hurried towards the downed visitor. This was to lend aid to the fallen. Ten more yards to reach him the Earth ceased to exist.

The end

Promise kept

The slaves were awful at it. Basically I felt that slavery must have been what they were suited to be. The war was going so badly for the redcoats that sinking so low as to tell the blacks if you help us fight a defeat these traitorous colonials, when we win those of you who fought on our side we will give to you your freedom

Some good number of the slaves stole over to the Brits. Their assistance with so much to them at stake was as nil.

The colonist greud stronger and won even more bottles. I did not at that time see it as I do see it in these times. Those revolutionaries wanted their freedom more than anything. That being reported I add this, but only slightly more than they wanted the Africans to not receive their own unfettering. I call it the Harvey Dent complex.

The colonist put the Brits in a hurried all out retreat. As the so called well trained British Red coated army's ran away hoping to stove off the loss of their lives. They abandoned the Africans and those left were again slaves to the now called Americans. That's it.

Some who are great historians certainly more knowledge than I declare that the Red coats could have won, but the Queen of England sitting at home on her thrown decided to lags the war on that issue.

For the real targets

Completed Sodoku board games cluttered every surface in the master bedroom. You could have facilitated a motorized leaf blower for a half of an hour to remove them, still there would remain enough for her two teen aged sons to say mom clean up your. That is if they dared. And dare they would not.

That clutter served for her very own personal purpose. Somewhere m various places hidden in the event of an intrusion were under, in between, behind those corrugated pieces of disconcerning game boards as was under her pillows, between her sheets and blankets, between the extra soft mattress and the double box spinged bed and on the floor under that bed were her toys.

It had taken her fourteen months of lonely days and nights before she could remember which of her choice of relief givers was in which little hide away. She now knows exactly what is where. Her most beloved one she had been unable to satisfy for two years and today she found he was ordered by Uncle Sam to be gone for a third tour of tour of duty in a row. It seemed to her that the United States National Guard was and still in the business of attempting to dislodge that part of a family which made the family a happy one.

The numerous shapes, sizes and colors were on her side. She unlike a plathern of many other displaced couples helped reinforce her resonance to remain a one man's woman. She would in no way disrespect her children nor disrespect herself. All first she composed herself to also not disrespecting her long. Long gone husband. In his second year away she drifted somewhat from caring about his respect or disrespect. It hurt her to think of him choosing to serve his uncaring government over a loving, hardworking and caring what seemed in being in an uncaring dilemma. Over his family.

Finding the heart shaped vibrator, the valentine's heart not the biological one her visage was beautiful to behold. Her eyes were most outstanding. Violet pupils with diagonal lines of dark and medium amber. Her eyeballs were pure white as white copy paper from her office copies. That whiteners due to the tears of two years of washing away the city dust and smog that belonged to her man but were owned by now washed clean pillows and sheets.

This one is those all to few real targets who fought the nobly, unlike the millions of other female and some stay home males that fought their overseas female enemies and won. With honor.

HEROES

Tuarius Got's funeral was going on. Many of those in attendance had come from either this town or that town. Some came whom were closer to him came from either this country or that. Gots while alive was the most prolific geologist on the planet. His educating students at the early ages from four or five years old gave those children insights that as they grew older helped colonize Saturn and Uranus a decade before his health started failure.

As every funeral of a truly loved one some personal speeches, epitaths really were recited. Earl Bailey, soon to be accredited a second doctorate gave his obience in the middle of those reciting.

Professor Gots predicted the Schlitz volcano. His prediction saved thousands of live. He had to the mountain on vacation. My mother and I were there on vacation. Well, I'll make this short. The magazines and other news services all told he was ignored until the last moments but he would not exist until all the women and children were on trucks and buses. He denied his seat numerous times. There were eight or ten other men doing similar acts as he.

My mom got the morning of evocation at the last moments. She told him I had gone off playing spelunking. They forced he on the very van. He went to find me and he did. I was scared as hell.

His experience led him to the top of mount Schlitz. I could see in his blinky eyes that he was trying to figure something out. Taken by my little hand he got on the top of a huge bolder and he had to help me climb it too. I was that little.

When the volcano erupted it erupted with a huge force and the sound closed my hearing for a full week. And a day and a half. We were directly under the blast.

Looking?·I think not. He figured it right. That bolder on that first demendous blast blew as high into air and about a mile southeast, directly into a part of the river that when the bolder landed in it way didn't completely sink and down. I am standing here to give him his testament. Take note. I said to give him his testament. And here it is. I was so little that during the flight on the rock I was to weak to hold on. I was falling. The only area his free had could take hold of me and keep me from falling to my death was my but, I could feel what he could not get a grip on my trousers. His face had that figuring look again. The next thing I knew was his two middle fingers forcing themselves through my baggy shorts into my anus's hole. Deep and hard. He looked directly into the eyes and calming face of Cherylie, his wife of two years and further elaborated Professor Gut's while saving my life broke my virginity that day. Then he said no more and honor to a fallen hero and friend and college professor lightly touched the top of mohogeny lined, stainless steel resting place. Entering into his advance wife's tended arms and small jiggly bosom.

I only wrote this story for you to allow you the awareness of what I heard as we guests were leaving. That self same wedded couple not knowing me as a writer her head totally lovingly affixed on her husband's chest arms around one another his head on the top of her head, she quietly murmured to him, when you were boy you were a little homo. A hint of a humorous smile. I haven't seen them since.

I did however see their picture of Home life's magazine cover. Ms. Universe and multi-billionaire husband six months into expecting baby boy scientist.

Tsk Tsk Tsk

Writing this early on a Saturday morning disturbs me. It is there a.m. plus four minutes. I have no avenue to sleep. For some stupidly odd reason the ghetto is when I have chosen to vacation. The hermits in ten year old autos are parked in various little one way dead end streets. In the future if your wife is late to come home or has gone away on the girls night out search that type of area. Forget the public parks. Cups in hopes of a successful free by petrol those.

Should she be an aged education with a young orally include stud one big mistake the unfamiliar younguns make often is to park by a grave yard. And get this under a city light yet. The closest guess I have come up with is he hopes her light brightness will make her invisible. As I have tried to get a closer look once believe me grandma you are easily soon

Some guys really don't mind a passes by getting an eye full. If the taste-taster can see the voyeur.

Do not worry bro, I will not tell your dad what I am hoping to get a tur..uh, what I saw her doing. Mummms the word. She's not even in her Volvo.

She started when seeing me. Probably dismantled his quiet peacefulness. His back was to the windshield and me but she was totally naked looking through that front window. Don't think she recognized as I approached from across the street in the dark, not wishing to negate my future chance of approaching that guys self game acquirement I hesitated my approach. I didn't just say that out loud, did I. I kinda hope that I kept that thought to myself. I am certain that would be almost like writing my intensions.

Now though years after what took place cannot help but wonder was she having him for a late dinner or an early breakfast. Stretching my wonderment maybe it was a din fast or on the other hand it was a breakner. No matter which of the two meals she was having him for, there is a little a missing.

Ahh. A way in maybe?

HMMMM

Hollywood as all other major movie studios missed the twist in this scene. Bligerence should be excised not rewarded.

She says to a supporting character "If you don't like it, go screw yourself." She usually has a share of top billing.

Here is want a answer on be, "Why do you give me only two options" biting her in. Then he gets her to bite. "Why do I have to go" She bites at that line. Then he plays her unzipping and taking it out. It lends better to the scene if he is small. She says and or thinks, pityfully small, now he reels her in by walking directly to her and stands there dangled in her face. Less than a inch separates her mouth from his manhood and says. "There is a fourth option."

THE WAY TO GO HOME

We won the championship earlier today. My ex called the hotel desk and left a congratulations. That spoiled perfect weekend. I have not heard from her before tonight since we were divorced. She divorced me for a couple good reasons. One was having women in the apartment while she was not home. It has been thirty two years in a couple months I would have liked an apology at sometime for that misconception of hers. The absolute one hundred percent truth never during my time married to her did I ever cheat. Not even one fucking apology.

The last two days Lo Li has been a sexual treasure. I guess that came with winning that championship. She has not stopped since we came in from dinner. That was over three hours ago. I read the exe's message while he was busy being busy. She does it and all the while her eyes. Those by horse colored eyes open, looking directly into face.

She is not like the Asians in the porn I have watched nor any other female. Most had their eyes closed until they occasionally glance upwards. Maybe for a moment or two and close the eyelids go.

Lo Li is scrumptiously hot body wise too. She has an aroma that seems as heavenly wafting as a man should wish for in a criticism.

I know she wants to move to Arabia with me when I go back home.

Wafting up to my proboscis is the very pleasantness of the well chosen by her the triple shot of warmed brandy and Benedictine from dinner. Mmmmm. Heavenly.

My penthouse calls out to us.

PRIDE OR PREJUDICE

America when I was twelve years old, fortified soldier of Russia made to defeat the top warrior soldier of the United States whom had not lost fight even when the numbers against him seemed insurmountable defeated his enemies. Always.

That time however the Russian fought the American one on one a fair fight. Well almost fair. The American super soldier who was being fought to standing draw used a weapon. The Russian with stood the weapon and continued to fight the contest hand to hand. The American writer put a twist to the story. The Red's coach and body builder suit the Russian in the back. He proclaimed, I created you to win against the capitalist. Not tie.

Decades later a similar story again the best American was pitted against a steroid fortified Russian fought hard. As did the American. As the American fought a little better in the letter part of the fist fight the tramer of the Russian slapped the champion of Russian in his face. He did so in front of a public audience mostly Russian in Russia. So much for the home crowd

In both stories though decades a part the creator of the yarns were both citizens good ole U.S.A.

Thieving to great power

Somehow getting these last few stories away from that abominable U.S. of A. has proved tedious at the least. Perhaps somewhere in these scripting of mine, printing to you and others is or are the cause or and the causes other nations are at a minimum, adding in your nations here to are viabilities of dismayances against the untied states.

For time is going ahead seemingly with a quickness she could possibly get away with it.

The U.S.A. a landmass historically entranced in thieves and noted thieveries.

Historically the country was burglarized from the now noted United Kingdom. Remember the revolutionary war, Holland and some others may remember a little continent called Africa. The U.S's part in that was large base expecting, via paying for the wares stolen by the small Dutch country. Do not feel too badly though "Nigerians and others". As vast as your home contenant was and still is, I can recall little Japan's islands government ruling over China's vastness. China however now rules over China. Not like that contenant that was the abode of your, how can I scrip this nicely? Evictions.

Maybe one day your pride will be, uh earned, real oh here is the word! Justified!!

That Armenian flag is awesome, double headed black eagle on an all red base. Yeah Armenia!

No more digressing from this stories total O.K.? Do not make me chastise you.

Did you know that the process of tar and feathering in the U.S.A. was stolen from Europe? Ahh, now that I find hard to believe. What do you tty to pull off here? You never heard of tar and feathering. Google it!

Did you yet get over your laughing spasms of the U.S.A's major part in stolen people aannddd slavery? Get over it already. I progress with this paper's title.

O.K. I'll sneak you one in here the living descendants of the nineteen thirty four Norwegian's have a nice sized little debt to collect on that heavy water incident. O.K again. So Germany stole it from them during occupation. The end result is thee atomic bombs were detonated over Japan's properties and Japan's people because the recipe for heavy water was ripped off from those self same tribesmen. O.K. a Germans.

In the case you are not familiar with the term "ripped-off", ripped-off is a synonym for stolen. You can relate I hope, that stolen is equal to theft in a past tense, erge those thieves. Yeah I am still referring to the U.S. of A.

Proving American's are thieves is very easy. Bare with me here "for-a-tie". In this part I shall attempt to cover something up making use of those whom I admire. I am being truthful. In accordance with my mind and my heart here I place the dedication to all the little nuputals (little girls) and all you little soldiers (little boys) I want your parents to share parts of the book with all of you. "If you're not careful you might learn something before its done."

Let the future prove I confess right here of the famous folks in this even shorter story, I just stolen from. Thank you, I trust your two thoughts aforementioned grown up in life's joyousness.

The end

FJORDS

Norway, Sweden and Finland form what my horse seeks in his mate everyday and I think most nights. I bet you will agree the two fjords they form align in your mind's annals when you view the three country's two waterways you will agree a healthy male horse as a healthy well may be a healthy horny male human should also. If I am not there I give you leave to show your own personal fjords. Mind now that when you do, he might fjord you. Enjoy your spaghetti.

LITTLE PEOPLE

Just one observation, if you do not. Aliens who have made contact with Earthlings in the past were probably all short in stature. If not then why are all the space movies made with only short humans. Center basketball guys and never in exploration movies. Shaquille's type are not being planned for the only two private space shuttles were privately owned. I saw nowhere was there seating for seven feet tall people. Allen !verso would feel right at home.

ONE MORE TIME PLEASE

She wanted to get up from bed almost pushing me from on top of and out of her. It took me years later to have a good answer for that. The two of us took over a decade to get in that position. I came to my senses that a couple days before I had a couple of ghosts floating in the area her attention was on.

My horse the one we were in a across the way from a colonial time grave yard.

Repetitive

I've had this writer's block so many times my designated allonym – blackhead.

BLACKEY

I know I wrote it down on my note pad. Where the splits is it? Count the pages in the book came by Blackey. My interest picked. What the hell can B be saying that for is my mental inquisition. It ran its course quickly eight, ten, twelve times. The cover notes seventy five pages. The spiral binding the pages have pieces of paper where something was torn cut inquisition over. Seventy three pieces. Two pieces missing. B has never been off point. This book is only unattended at home and in the precinct. My mind gagged as I went over the home situation. B played me as a fiddle. Here, I accepted the two pages. You know the same as I do. The office is tainted. Do not slip again. I do not want to have to watch your back at your home. Again the inquisition home? Is B telling me something? I can now wondering as I check the information on the two now loosely in place two sheets of paces, do I need to use my backup piece. It is an unregistered eighty percent.

Reading the report aloud to the major I read the vio was found spiked to an oak tree three feet from the grass in Forced Sex is a crime park at two zero two a.m. this morning dated October thirty nine teen fifty three. Description on scene body was found impated to the tree by fire railroad spiked. All of the spikes were fully through the body and into the tree. No part of the spikes protruded except the heads were able to be seen. The bodies frontal part was to the tree truck, Arms were spread apart outward from one another as like spread wings. Both were impelled between the Aina and the radius bones. A third spike went into the back of his scrotum into and severing. Partially severing his penis while still into its skin and as the forearms the rest of the spike impaled into the oak. Both that is the left and the right schilies tendens were cleanly slices through with what is probably a razor blades to the depth of past the ankles bones. The feet then bent upward parallel of the oak tree between the tree and the shins. That is both feet and then impaled with a railroad spike both feet front their insteps through the feet pads and impaled into the oak tree and again railroad spikes were implemented for the implement. End of report. Your conclusions if any inquired the major? Clearly a suicide. Sir.

Our shifted ended and the commander threw us out of the office. B and I were about to head our separate ways and I got that you just had to go and do it didn't you look from B. What? I hunched my shoulders to my partner. Will you stop pissing all over the Chief. Remember when you reported to him that nine eleven was most likely a mass suicide? I will never will against that type of repose from B.

B's cost collar pulled up due to the fall chill and headed. B is married to the city's Chief of police. She is the absolute best. Safety forces me to tale a quick glance over my shoulder to watch my partner. Everything's good. Me I am on my way to Doc's the sexiest nude bar in New York State.

FAT

Fat people. You do not get to love them. I owe one of them. The one I owe does not know of my debt to her and she never will. The purker must be over three fifty, at about five feet three. A picture, the frame is too small for it to fit inside, when I wide-eyed her before I tuned her out my mind was made, like granite.

I am six feet and at the sighting was at a scaled one eighty. Out of my fifteen fights I was fourteen and one with twelve K O's one dreadful loss by decision and one unanimous win. My future had to be in heavier classes.

How she helped is if her body looked like that and did I forgot to mention she gluttonously stuffing her face was keeping at it. I should be able to of my diet and gym it up. Now almost a year later I am at two sixty. I was a purker. At six feet tall two sixty's view is still svlet.

Come on three zero eight, may be nine. Soon upcoming break up. The depot her mouth stuck at as far as humanly possible looking like the top of a duck's bill. Her right and left arms muscle development made all notice body builders strenuously caring heavier weights and more often.

WHY SHOULD WE HAVE RE-ELECTED

Mama bear was giving one of her boy cubs the lesson. When you have your hand in the mouth of the lion, you don't jerk it out.

Me not being a fan of the States President Biden, that lesson would not even come to mind when he had a chance to diplomeize the possible necessity of a few extra days may arise and with the new Afghany governments allowance all the American's retreat from the Afghany territory will be assured. We the people of USA request your assistance here.

Instead we all now know what that anus pore said to the Afghan President. Very shortly hence from his inflammatory threat the first bomb now made a viable peaceful retreat an illusion and caused Afghany and American deaths and wounded.

A few small words from a powerful though even smaller man. Does the call for impeachment come from the Democratic Party of which Biden is a member murmur and resonate over and over murderer!

HELLO IT'S ME

It has been an easy day. Most times on this day of the week round about this time guilt slams at hard. Honestly it should too.

If not for what happened, misery loves company would apply. To be particular the stand-by phrase "You know how when..." is negated. Guilt get out. I owe this too to my own self. Seems reporting doctor's bad conduct is investigated by the American medical association does get investigated. Short time ago Doctor Rajes Gupta was reported doing unhealthy activity behind my back when I was his patient. Seems using a nostril inhaler that was empty and refilled with urine, faces, mint and oil and then purposely squirting the contents of it on a patients back and also sticking the point of a needle used to inject a pain retardant in the bottle and afterwards injecting it in a patients lower lumbar is a serious violation of medical ethics. A physician found guilty by the A.M.A. will lose his license and his office closed immediately.

You have the details, so in shelf I went to visit my pain management doctor today and I could get in, nor could anyone else. Sweet satisfaction.

DIVORCE

The relaxation was needed. Since the divorce his duties almost triples. Morgan used to have a run of the southern slave end of the busy. She had her mother his now divorced wife Kelisia run the slave business in Delaware, Massachusetts and in Pennsylvania.

His lawyers get him everything except two and a quarter million in gold bullion that went to Kelisia. Morgan choose to transverse with her too.

He is now hiring for the sugar and tobacco fields. The foreman, the only one who carried on with him Rhedt oversaw the slaves on the cotton plantation, the largest the southern states had to offer.

The word that the south is definitely on it's way to ceceding from the United States. Being South Carolina's first man in the renown category his vote was already recorded.

The old short fat Nigerian's head was finally able to let the shaft's release be. He had given his permission only minutes for after Georg Buchweiser had been announced and entered. He bided Georg be seated. Guided by her owner her mouth engulfed Buchweiser, as the younger clerk slave changed position and his mouth took in the meet the women had been ordered to change from.

The two men talked for the next two hours and then some. Both of the slaves were then sent to the slave quarters. Had either of them had developed a thirst over the horse, their thirst without the slaves members been quenched.

Nothing was dergure. The blacks would tonight have their near end holes plunged by their owner, when done with the two as usual he would sleep with his member in the mouth of young Hottie, fourteen years old.

The cracked old Mandigo Joseph would stand ready beside the bed all night with the row hide should her mouth even by way of accident let go of him.

He would have the nightmare of Morgan and Kalisia doing the same with the girl slave for each.

Idi Amin

I really did not wish to go back home. I took so Hack there and for no good reason. I do not live in Africa. I have never been to Africa. Other places I had traveled to after I took as much ridicule as I could take dismissed me with malice. They all must have known I was not the caught and executed criminal whose name I share. Home was worse. Here I landed and the name meant nothing to these people. They had never heard of him I had a good job. I community recognize me for what I was and had established while here now I am called to return home to nastiness and ridicule. Both are undeserved. There are great difference between he and me. Him I will not even think God rest his soul even when only alluding to his atrocious activities. I have no desire to return to my home country, especially my home area. It wrecked me before I had left and those people I knew who were aware I was not him still shirked me out of my nights. I go.

THANK YOU

Wondrous are the little ones. My thought every time and every park I have gone visiting asserting necessity and attaining it with peace of mind.

Pigeons, sparrows and robbins of the avian genous: squirrels and ants of their own kinds after a few years of acquaintance advance to me straight away even lighting on the picnic table and or chair I have decided to roost for that day. Not dis-coordinating and giving no cause to fear along with breads, doughnut, cakes and nutty trial mixes allow me their wanted company. It is soothing.

The other major advancers have singularly and in multiple various numbers have ever a few summers brought to me an end of anxiety. Teachers arrive with pre-schoolers. Parents accompany their offspring on visits to nature also enjoying the plethora of treats sold devouring ice creams, waffle fries various sandwiches and salads and so on. Pleasant experiences mostly.

I watched the little ones over the years trying to catch a bird or a squirrel. The squirrels know the little ones cannot catch them and move so quickly as to discourage the kids from trying. It does not work. They try every time. The rodents as per to a low branch in a near tree and observe the disappointed head back to their parents. I think that they must be laughing. The happy elders assuage their young ones failures with sufficient glee. The unthinking children are safe from the would be trophies claws and excessively strong front teeth.

The sparrows on the other hand play a game of. I have no idea of what they call it. It goes in this manner. Smiles on the little human faces. Stretched out forward arms and fingers and thumbs opening and closing pursue them. The little birds hop away but only a short distance half turn their heads around as the child stops the chose. The birds stopping the chase is renewed. The happing away continues. This stop and go pursuit would continue endlessly as the birds sensing not to go to far from the protective parent(s) before going out of a short rage of comfort they sparrows are to stay close to the adults protective watch. The odd part is the children's parents become aware of the birds helping four toed feet are assured inside and only verbally wronglee their offspring to eat, ride the carousel, play mini golf or its time to go home.

The pre-kinder gardener teacher's are only a little different in their routine snack time over if they have one then the short trek to the gated community for their particular group play chase, ride swings, monkey bars and or whatever.

So rest peacefully dads at work you are covered and the only old prevent there is me. Neither God nor I will rest fury should the peacefulness be quelled. That it about it and you're welcome.

Just one more thing. I have wanted to do that Columbo line with a meaning to it for years and years. Bring news paper for your pups. Bags in a place where people sit and play on the grass leaves residual dog droppings unless you do allow your pop to relieve on the news papers first. Gals, heggy.

DISAPPOINTED

Sam was infected by a guys blood by accident whose own blood was accidentally gamma irradiated. The original irradiated victim when emotionally challenged into a certain manner metamorphically changed into a ten foot tall muscle bound cyolopsed eyed maniac behaved danger to all that encompassed his vicinity. He had turned into and out of the extremely powerful monster like being over decades and had become world renown

On November 12th twenty twenty a spark of the strength Sam inherited through the transference of Gamma irradiated blood.

Knowing what had transpired in his system and having who the transference come from expecting changes in his mental and in his physical self proved proper. Though the event would seen be self recognized as the most eventful occurrence in his life he still was awed at his reading the story of Feodore Vagsilver and spouse Valentina. She gave birth twenty seven times yielding sixty nine children. Both parents were Russian in heritage.

The expected occurred. Massive covertness. Only his hair on his head physically changed. The hair now green also grew a foot in length from his normal crew cut style. Those were viewable emotionally, chemically or physically, it will oppress one mental acuity to end a definite decipher what his strength and endurance enhancements were he capable in understanding his cyclopean benefactor's destructiveness, he sought the way to temper himself.

Ten barely endurable later later Frian Michael's teachings and guidance assisted him in his success. The two believed. His final test a smooth stone not a quarter once in weight. Use your full control. You can get it done the monk spoke to him. Split the stone directly in even halves. Some puzzlement shortly crossed Sam's braw. You can get it done the Monk started then he calmly place the pebble of stone on a large stone boodle.

Sam's hand and arm raises into a ninety degree chopping position. Swifty with all but unseeable the motion touched the stone very slightly. Directly in half lied the two pieces slightly wobbling as though a pimple hand ball had been decided, half ball in mind.

Hours later as Sam departed the Himalayan seclusion he saw on an airport news screen the reporting of a massive tsunami on its way to urope heading towards and expected to go as far as Central Africa south and Brazil and Colombia Southwest and the east coast of Canada and the United States of America southwest to the tip of Florida, Cuba and Puerto Rica only hours ago. He simply quietly verbalize "tsk."

He never would realized the fullness of his powers used only hours past that the vibrations of the spitting of that small stone caused that some reported event.

Twenty one hours later with a single left hook unleashed by him on his gamma irradiated benefactor lied flat on his back. Knocked out.

I wrote this parody only because of my disappointment of the owners of the story and the characters parodied have not moved an event where the irradiated monster like here fought an alien and was soundly thrashed by the alien. The offshoot of the gamma irradiated monster-hero was totally neglected. How could you have not missed that.

I am an Earthling and I do not like it when others make me loose to an alien!!!! Get it?!?!

CANDY WARS 1

Where you aware that there is more than one Valentine's Day cherib? Your answer to that question will probably that you never gave it thought. As had I. one night before Thanksgiving sitting in a strip joint I overheard a few guys all in business and ties pissing the dancers twenty's and fifty's as they drank doubles sooth, Rye and vodka, I got lap danced through three girls. Took hours of my tens I realized a couple of things. First three hundred of my dollars got my trousers drenched. Another they never stopped shaving down doubles one right after another. On the path to my realization a heard then talking over and over about gibberish of Martha Clause and her husband Santa having had put out a planet wide alert how his wife went missing a few days. None had found her. A bunch of businessmen. If they were the bosses and rival companies had seen and heard them than the stock market would take a deep hit tomorrow morning. My mind gave me a wink and I found all that booze, easily a couple fifth each they had drank and were still slashing down, not one of them mispronounced a syllable.

I even tried to call them nuts somehow and I know how, I won't bring it up they talked how the corporate offices all over made billions of profits selling candy, cards, gifts and the like in their own cherib images. They were I guess because the only paying them any attention were the things hoping to rob them, the girls trying to get them in the rooms under the club and me.

I did not follow then when they left. A few of the thugs departed about a half minute after they left.

What they said just before leaving stayed in my ear. Let's go tear into Martha some more the other guys a probably bored with her by now, said the blue three pieces George style suit. Might as well. I'll get her to polish my nob three or four more times before I ran her in that adorable cherry pit of an ass, said the grey two piece Italian out. The third in what looked like a white silk Cardin said my bottom can use some more French from her. Her tongue is nice. And those sweet lips. May as well top her little ass again to. It won't be little any more when Mark and Jewiidhia get here with their crews from the Ozzak's.

INTELLIGENCE THROUGH EVOLUTION

Her funds now rest a short distance from being empty and she a step or so away from homelessness in more ways than one.

The landlord arriving as per his world hands to he two long mouse traps. Each was a perforation containing two traps, white plastic holding a very sticky glue. The mouse walks on it gets stuck and dies. That was the thought of her landlord anyway. When she saw the type of poisons he handed he's back she held her concepts.

I am paying an idiot eight hundred fifty dollars a month for a furnished room and private bath. No knowing human being would waste good earned funds on that type. No self respecting mouse would get on one of those. They are at best an archaic uselessness. Then came the motion, may be a new born.

Her brain led her correctly cut of the four mice the neighbor whom had moved into the room next to her leased toilet, toilet yes, there was no bath only a sink, toilet and showering room with self controlled as was the bedroom baseboard heat.

The conversation with the dollar plus store clerk put into her mind that the wooded snap traps she requested were too probably archaic.

The story I was told complimented my own experience. Keep setting the same trap. Only throw the mice away. I knew a girl who caught forty mice that way.

Six years earlier I was renting small bedroom in a ghetto just above the poverty line area. I was on a missing persons case. Saw mice. One bit me in my slumber. Next thing the mice knew was a morsel of nourishment next to the floorboard I had seen them travel. That night the food was gone. For two days I kept baiting- the trap then on the third day I figured word spread. Free food! I set the to a contraption. One down. Sadness but glee inside the slightest of smirk. Get rid of the care ass. Reset, at the end of the week no more answers to the question. No more mice to make it simple.

The clerk's story and my experience jibed. I have but one half grown to adulthood.

The set wooden contraption is under my bed. Having seen the rodent since I got it.

THROUGH THE YEARS

I am the for mort authority an robotic life overthrowing our planet. It is and was my own doing. The situation all of are facing is my own doing. Safeguards to avoid your fate were ignored by the former authorities I pleaded be put in place were at the world meeting denied due to my own misbehavior. In short our exile from our planet and forced by mechanical technology to be adrift into this firmament all of us can put the entire bonus on me.

Owning up to my discrepancies I tell you this. I am the only human alive with realization of our needs of assertiveness in the voids ahead and assurances of the guaranteeing of mankind's future existence.

The Democrats refused my past warnings only for reasons of the marital aversions committed by their mothers and wives in my bedroom. The Democrats refused my warnings and this is where we are.

We need to elect are to get it right. The mothers and wives of the Republican party and I have also played "It was only for a little while." While also. They need to vote with you and I and have me lead our deportment from the Earth by the robots both political parties ordered into existence. I told them not to create them. Those disavowed my knowledge and we lost our planet.

Vote for me. And we live.

After the speech in the sleeping quarters that mouse trap had not snapped. It had new been almost one hundred hours. What was it eating? Every bit of edible supplies are accounted for- looked up fight. There are no double incisions bites on my body. I have found no visible avenue of retreating from this room. Somehow it had gotten in, goes my mentality. The bit of fresh fish fillet had dehydrated so I rebated the word and brass thing-a-msh-jib.

REEEAALLY

Did you ever see an action movie where there is one of the gun fight scenes that reminds you of the old television show with miss Arline Mae Beller as Sally star, host of Popeye Theatre when a hand gun shoots out say maybe one hundred bullets. Without reloading. I have, If you did than write to the promoters and complain. Do not let it get by. Them trying to idiotize the public is one of my two pet peeves.

You probably don't give a flying whatever, so here is my second pet peeve. The best the country has to offer and the best the mafia has to offer get the call to blast the star away and when the time comes up this most deadly accurate shootist either hits the targeted victim in the leg, or the arm and let's not forget the complete miss. Add to that as greet an assassin sent to do the hit is folded by a wait for it, wait for it mirror image.

Heres another one the federal government agents, no matter what government shoot and hit the window sill, the top of a wall their opponent is jumping over. These are the best marksman in the world and

You not only do not get the target because you chose the time to shoot just as they move but you are good enough to hit a window sill or a wall. The assassin is great at hitting walls and window sills you don't aim at.

Oh well I guess being lonesome is not one of my failings.

LET IT BE. LET IT BE. LET IT BE

Naabeeho's people have been at this for hundreds of years. Now today January first twenty six hundred and one P.C. the achievement is but a day away.

The lands awarded them are of the most fertile with vastness of sweet clean waters and mountains of providence in numbers their people have only until this century were as numerous as their songs of praise.

Let none stand in the way of noncompliance.

Since the sol galaxy was destroyed and the moment of survivors departure before its armagedon only the Novajo has prospered so competently. Without dependence on the new ragtag members of the few surviving ethnicities.

The Irish and Scotts gone. The Brits Japanese and ninety eight percent of Italians and Africans good. They were the first to die out. Outer space darkness, cold and various dust storms along with black lightning and asteroids get them within a year of escaping the machines.

Asians and Spaniards survive numerly as do the Naabeeho's but not nearly close to living conditions though average in comparable.

The areas are fertile years. Food can and does grow in abundances the few types the land yields.

All the others scraping bottom and their numbers are few in comparence. No nationality abides with another. In today's time pride is truculent. Obstreperoveaness there is no tolerance for it.

Mankind of any ethnicity has no weapons. When force to leave after losing the wars to critical intelligence no ·weaponry was allow mankind. That was a term of survival afforded its existence

I WIN

Her bra was put on where her panties were supposed to be and v-ice versa. In her hasty departure done stealthily as getting out her professors bed room was unplanned. His wife was in a guestroom when she and the professor arrived hours before the professors wife's lover heard the couple and quickly departed creapingly.

Neither of the back stabbing married couple was ever aware of the others discrepancy.

The first time the clothing designers had dared to present the upcoming fashions in full view of the buying public was chaneey. Giving the show in Numibia and broadcasting on the worldwide broadcasting channel not only gave view to the buying public giving them a look on what was to be liked, accepted, loved and frowned upon without the benefits of collusion of the seller's influences of what styles were to become popular, still it went over well. The designers for once did out do the necessities for successful immediate and future sales.

The greatest item to become purchases order over the web Meryl's undines. It surpassed the former big underwear item of a decade age. Meryl a former abductees in sex trafficking abused and raped over ten years before the federal police were forced to investigate and rescue her. The idea was a thong underwear where the bra could not be differentiated from the panty and vice versa. It broadcast you could conceivably easily go to you. Corporate meetings with your bra on your vagina and would not be knowing it she called it the cheat suit.

She went back home the next morning on her private oxicorp four hundred twin engine twelve seat private compartment lean jet.

MacGivenci Ogk, her husband had his laugh when she entered their area he was wearing the bra on his midsection and the Party to the set around his neck.. I'm ready. He said. They collapsed into the accompanying position.

CANDY WARS 2

Their ragdoll could not move on her own. Exhaustion over took weeks ago. Still no stopping the onslaught the evil cherabim. Martha was so out of it her mew like moaning die out ten day past.

Bugs was at roger's newly opened club. It debuted three days ago and Jessica's singing wowed all patrons. Dolly, Reba, Taylor, Jennifer, Lucinda and LeAnn all attended opening night others did come in and out but the big names were being warned off starting from the first night. The word was creeping out. A war was coming and a replacement for easy was now due to necessity being sought. Easy was the one and only Easter bunny.

Easy was reported missing a possible kidnap victim months ago. In country's around the world pieces of easy were being allowed to be found. No eyes nor ease's cotton tole had surfaced. It was later noticed that Peter had become missing even before easy.

That is why talent agents were now telling their stars to stay away from Roger's.

Some helpful slicksters did not want to adhere to the warnings. Jessica's body was an absolute bomb. Not the kind of bomb that decimated the night club when the last guest had the limousine take them to breakfast.

Roger and bug's body parts were found as far away as an eight of a mile. Jessica, Charo and Dolly went to nathans for turkey frank further.

Part one: Santa Clause part two easy Bunny:

U-2

The specifics of being a parent is first to remember that at one time in your life you probably looked upward as you contemplated, how can I get over on you. The you usually was supposed to be young adult people, your mom and your pop. Some who were fortunately unfortunate or unfortunately fortunate in only having one tall adversary to temporarily overthrow a will. If however you were one of those with four or six tall people to undermine, then you should know what complete futility feels akin to - you. Grands when in fortitude with their sibling or siblings will most assuredly end in your utter and her crews dominating victory over you, so be wise when grands are about another day.

If you smart you will get them, all six of them to become a sixth seventh of us and complete the number from a fraction to a whole number. It will make for while you are still in your childhood mind you better if not more and if you are extremely compromising to the sixth's will along the read to birthday and Christmas gifts- both!

The exclamation point here is assured but smoothly low in volume.

If I had know of candy wars first one, than I still would inform the advice you have been given a few sentences ago still holds true, but lean a big bit more towards your natal-day.

I told some once they have a leak. Read on you will comprehend the aforementioned even if you do not recall it when you do. Trust me now and further ahead.

Don't believe me yet? But you should, how many perfect attendance awards did you get while you were in grade school. Your parents did not get wise to you if you had no E's and only one - maybe two D's, those missing and late days are numbered on that same card. You duped your own self. Your child may be duping their own selves right now aaannnddd U 2.

Memories not so sweet sweet

When I pulled up to the bank there crime tape borders blocking the sidewalks. TD was on the corner. The corner was at that time closing the back doors on the enclosed corps.

Should my peepers not be deceiving me the room to be D.O.H was no pauper. Since one had either not covered or discovered the victims wrist and on it were two thin intricately filigreed designed pale white jade wristlets. I saw them. Should I find his family as I suspect will be part of my investigation, I will see to it the family has them and not some unscrupulous city employee. It happens a lot. Families deprived of a dear departed's possessions and it turns up in an employees dresser and or their bank accounts.

Not once until this day had I thought ascertain where the white jade was purchased which does pic at me as to since first learning white jade existed I have been to jewellers even Asian jewelers who had the doorway to all jades. I was about thirty years old then. I am in my late sixties now. Unlike the green stuff, white jade is very valuable and extremely rare.

When talking to homicide I found the vio's name was the Terriya. I made sure the detectives recovered his wrist bands from the ambulance driver's. needless to say the two were not arrested. Not following the transport to the morgue could have depleted the chances of the window recovering her husband's expensive trappings. But that meant nothing to me when Mrs. Terriya asked the authority detective Iesa Jablons, were in Desi?

The scene went ballistic when none knew of Desi, her three year old daughter.

They had walked his young daughter through the parks play ground on the way to deposit funds.

My mind conjured up a photo of the child I had never before seen. If your mind can't take it don't read any more of this even shorter story.

The three years old girl would probably be found a day or so later, may be even later that day, if found alive.

In my third eye were pictures of dark browns perpetrators. Drawing on my only Asian child kidnap experience I had.

I never did find the name of the kid. She was just a month over two years old playing outside of the house where lived. Her five year old sister was with her. Two black adults in their early thirties walking through the block picked her up in one of their arms and walked away with her. Her elder sister saw it happen. A minute probably went by before her analyzation realized tell mom as the soon to be kidnapping rapist turned the corner at the black with child in arms of one of them.

The mother now out of her apartment going up and down the full of the city block then quickly around the block. Fifteen minutes later. A frantic fifteen minutes to her. I believe she returned with her raped two year old. Blacks, again came to my mind. You can bet when their street people hear of what happened they would be full of glee, quietly rejoicing.

To this day the police in Philadelphia, Pennsylvania's ninth district police never even sought the two men.

Desi was found dead three days later. Anus ripped by sexual intercourse vagina severely bruised and swollen shut. Mouth violated so badly that the back of her gums and throat was ragidly raw.

Do not I ask you call me a racist. True I am prejudice. The story of the three year old child is however one hundred percent true.

No tiny premeditation

Once the me. told me the reason for the twenty year old blonde bombshell socialites death the method of demise was a matter of insignificance you might say. Ingestion of poison over a period of about a month.

Deduction of how out of my way the who proved to be impossible. There was surely more than a killer. The acts were done with intent. The only way it could be done was the murderers had to be aware of each others act or act. They each used the same method.

Check the victims travels backward for thirty days when the poisoning's outset frame about few people traveled the same territory more than a day or two of the thirty and none on those plural days more than once during the vic's time of travel.

There were thirty different DNA, identified on the vic's body and in the vic's respiratory system and blood test. Most of it completely unidentifiable due to skin cleansing creams and various antifungal soaps used by the dead woman.

Various greases, urine and stool from human and animals but no way to identify the DNA without a match on file from the couple our came up with.

I figured out the taking of showers killed her. The poison was distributed on her through various nasal inhalers by squirting the contents of the labs findings along with rat poison and rodent poisons and such.

Spraying the inattentive vic attached to her hair and skin, the shower ran it in her mouth and up her nostrils.

In the last month she had come m close proximity of more than ten thousand people she didn't even know. The busy streets. The trains, buses and taxies to work and home. Add in the club life every Friday night and a Saturday when she took no one home on Friday night.

Finding the specific killer(s) impossible. Case closed.

A PIECE OF THE PUZZLE

City police officer O'hanrahtly and McDrourke stood on the northwest corner of Butch Lane where the lane intersected Shesgayetti street, in the millionaire business district of a major city in a first world century. The names of the lane, street, city and country are of no importance. Most major countries fit the category.

Hey officers how are you guys? Their minds questioner but only a little besides if there is some criminal hiding in public in to keep from being noticed puts himself directly in front of us. The old adage goes if you want to do something wrong do-it in front of the police. If he's a fool than we'll yet him sooner or later they rely on the standby just in the event it is as seems, a cordial greeting.

Half-ass okay's bluet out in word by one of them. A sideways tilt of the head by the other.

Great story healthy he says crosses Shesgayetti and heads into tight clicks, the area savings bank.

The two officers mount their ninety nine percent identical city issued ten speed interceptor all terrain bikes. Both take notice of an European Indian adult male and a little girl of his nationality slowly walking hand in hand. Peaceful as peaceful can be for nor. One of the officers however even though he progresses on ward with his assigned route for today has a slight bothersome feeling. The father and child's life would have tuned out differently had petrol man Blonque paid attention to his psycho. His not approving that quiet but not silent little voice than he would still be a member of his country's most elite covert weapons team.

Blasters were going in to retrieve two stolen nukes. The plans at gone over they attack. Has gone to plan perfectly the theses and guardians of the two bombs make a hastey withdrawal carrying away two packages in an attempt to get the cargo away from the elite recovery assassins, the blasters decimate the even that plan attain the two packages and make an unstoppable withdrawal getting to their planned rendezvous and head back to their own country.

The new officer on his route for today and then elite retrieval specialist blonque sticking to the team's plan ignored his psycho.

The enemy had outsmarted the brains who were the former of this retrieved. The actions to regain the nuclear bombs was naturally anticipated and the backer to not lose the advantage of having the bombs hidden while the attempt to run away with fatties was administered. And it worked. Bloques psycho again had been shuttled into ignorance.

HER BEST FRIEND HAS A FICKLE FINGER

In their sites only partially. The need to accomplish their part of the mission depended now on her moving forward the high back of the chair impeded what would be the trajectory.

Her appetite satiated and the pre- pangs of hunger again began to ravage her mind. Ten more courses lie on floor only yards in front of her. Her mouth cozed saliva out of each side and down cheeks to the chin that now drizzled onto her enormous twins.

She stood and her seventeen hundred pound frame walked dancingly towards the nine men and one female child. Gleefully preparation caressed her mind. Four elephant tranquillizer darts took but a few moments to put her prone on the while marble slabs put there by her maintenance crew. Refurbishment is to take place tonight. Her entresol's new makeup would put the kremlind in enviousness

Her cannibalistic tang would have to accept a serious impediment. Imprisonment with shackles and chains until she starved to death.

Since so when she ate people she used a recipe book for uncooked foods the ten saved souls voiced their gratitude numerous on every accepted invitation from public media. Only one the adults stopped the police. He had let a little child the only would be victim under eighteen years of age let it slip to a radio producer at WKBK in hells kitchen, New York that her guardian had been sexually molesting her since she was four years of age when he hooked up with her single mother.

The child started the outing of her tormentor by saying if my mom had only went back to where they had moved from then she bet her father whom she never would not have let him and she cut off. Since the producer overheard the conversation that was guided towards the prisoners that were with her when she was saved.

Her mom was called to the station and the police took it from there, the eleven years old girl smiled over and over that night even while on her knees, hands folded.

Prelude to the Candy War

One on one. That is how the females met fifty meetings in all. One for each territory one Siolian one Asian. There was but one Ajenda. The same for every meeting. Decided the majority of yeses than all fifty would follow. The same for neys. Only a twenty five twenty five would bring war between the groups. If war or agreement it would be honored globally.

Since these meeting were secret you may never be told the reason for the meetings under pain of my death.

It is not solely that those females are vicious and venomous but all of them have a bee in their bonnet directed towards me. Letting the word out on them that they are the country's most successful criminals, made them greater malcontents than my ex that one really got them so angry they wanted to raise their leg up into the air and take a piss.

I comprehend why they got so angry. I did prove the point I made that men, their men were dolts in the past. There men are dolts in the present and though I they more than likely stay the way they are and will be dolts in the future.

Laws written read that one cannot benefit from criminal activity even if one does not commit the actual crime(s). even al Capone's consort never went to jail but lied very much in vogue on Copone's criminal gains. Many more significant others live plus still live modos operan the same you technical support i.e wives are still irritate about my informing. So you little know how violent and unforgiving the ferns are I try to get on their side that pays little attention in as I called all then criminals wives not mentioning - by way of this scripting those of them not married and getting dinners, jewelry, apartments, cars and equivalent booty from their boyfriend illegalities. Them insane, crazy females took unbridge to me saying I was trying to cut them out of their historic due.

Finally my will became impecunious. I mentioned it in written words and get into their concern anyway. Seems some of the boyfriend spending their criminally procured money on the significant others were also wedded.

They were clever. Let us attack the very day he was brought into being said an Asian woman. Mind clicking a remembrance of a large order of valentine flowers and candy to that bitch Iletta Devatte a way to go with an attack on Halloween began the go ahead for the candy war.

Partner's, Buddies and Pals

Cheletta always was aware of what was happening in her kitchen. She made aversians to any impropriety from cleanliness to late deliveries she as all the servent heads kept her port of the banks sixty million dollar stone antibian tight.

B her full name Anjobeth banks had a little car going with all the head servants it was playful for all and fun mostly for B. she was four years old going on a joyful ten. And those thanks giving hay dinner turkey shaped just removed from the oven soon to be decorated after cooling cookies smoked great. The one in the right corner on the cooling rack was the target.

Choletta day ago when making up the menu kept her smile knowing the battle with B is on. Choletta had deciphered out knowing B well the target would be the coded pudding or the cookies. She knew the battle would be battle of wits and timing. B would be aware Choletta had to the cooking station and check on other parts of the kitchen. Choletta out of the kitchen was off knits. Out of the area where the treats would be would be no fun. Skills could not be tested when backs where in another area. The child is a snack attack genious. Getting caught once two years ago choletta still was not sure B had not set her up. Sure the slices of marble iced cakes was dampened but the fresh strawberry filled, lemon water ice covered jello was deplected by two. B's best friend Angela both the same age who died in a yaght adventure later was in attendance that day.

B says hello everybody as she enters the vastness of the sectioned off seven times kitchen area, easy waves and glad tidings to the little body full of love, joy and respect. Now in the area where the dance of the chosen snack begins. Choletta gains her hearts joy. Wiping hand sanitizer from her palms B is surrounded by the head of the kitchen staff with a warm and cautiously soft engulfing hear hug Choletta is a huge woman over six feet five inches tall with a thick four hundred seventy two pound and surprisingly sexy looker. Choletta's smooth face caresses B's long brown never been cut hair. B is a gile. A girl in love with Choletta her heart beats to a love fast thump. My cookie awaits. Choletta tries to not let B know the is now aware the target is the cookie.

Neither really looks forward to dislodging from the others warmness, but employee duties take president and for B quietly the plan is put in motion. Cookies as a little shag character one frame her thoughts.

Thether had the stuffing finished and called her official stuffing taste tester B over to refrigerator for the official taste tester's okay. Thether never put together a dish B had not raced over to parents B get a second taste after her eyes lie up. The fluffy flavored bread was impeccable in presentation but it was suppressed by its goodness.

The cookie exited with Anjobeth the unstated role success was to get pass the kitchen's mistress to any part of the house where the treat was not.

Elett called out B and beckoned the kitchen head. Time to pay of chimes B's voice.

One second child goes Choletta, them closes the call on her cell phone. And stands directly face to face with the cookie producing winner.

B went into the dinning room and sat at the dinner table after Choletta had taken her half of the turkey shaped cookie.

To my Nineteen hundred DOLLAR RING

Not right now. Humnh? Was the question to my better half. I continued, what do you, not right now? I see you watching that fifty dollar gold eagle for coin collectors. I know you want one- some. Pure gold cost of four hundred dollars a piece. A collectors item. Then they tell you the value has to go up. No investment went up more than gold in seventy years. Here is what they are not telling you babe. Gold took hit last month and went down in value. I nod I am slithered to she looks up and nods.

QUANTUM THEORY

Jessie vanking is in the most important conference of his king is in the emperors suit. The emperors rent for thirty five thousand dollars an hour. It is definitely not for the small fry business nor is it for the small fry businessman. The second titan at the meeting is Martin Jackson, they are on the phone with Elvis Jackson, he is not related to Martin Jackson.

The two have just ended giving Elvis Jackson the negative report.

Elvis Jackson presses the yellow button. It is one of three button on his watches wristband. The tree each have a permanent designation. This watch's cost even some Arab Emirates cannot afford.

He gives the two billionaire his regrets and notates to them why he chooses not to adhere to their wishes nor to their requests

The rumbling increases to deathening creshende.

The first responders fought the collapsing towers dust, fire and wreckage crashing to the ground. The twin towers in the very near future would cause a war to breakout. The reason terrorism.

Elvis Jackson's one reason for the commercial air line crashing into the second tower was to cover up the other jet liner crashing into the second tower Elvis Jackson left nothing uncovered even the fact that Marishka Jackson, his wife was at that same time having a midday nosh in the first of the twin towers.

Rick James day died along with Marishka. James was the nosh Marishka was on her padded having.

HERE'S TO P.B.R

In two years living together her knees now have thick calooses from the time spent on then pleasuring her mate orally. More than five hours every day. Her upper shoulder blades were in about the same condition from the arching her mid section balancing her arched body with the upper shoulders, top back of her head where baldness had appeared from the contact of the various carpets and on her flattened feet were blistered callouses also. She did not release the sun on bright sunny day. Clear as a cloudless tens starlit night went wavy. The sound become crackling with static

Checking the antenna caused no change. Flipping around the sir station to station did not help. The cell phone call to the television cable company revealed it was not the company and probably satellite disruption was at that very being checked, before the bar keep hung up on the troubleshooting technicians the state cessed as did the wavy lines the screen went black.

The mug of beer in a frosted mug and half loaded with shaved ice now contained a quarter mug of shaved ice. A second mug appeared in front of the military man. T.V's gonna be out for a while. Announced the travern owner and his gate in walking away calling his wife on his flip down was slow and purposeful. It has every appearance of being filled with exhaustion.

Double the cost of a mug was left on the counter. The bar door's spring closed as the only customer in the bar way on his way with his own reasoned personal gate all his own.

About the Author

My history is in my books, so to all you other authors try this on for size.

I take imaginative liberty.

My mom was Venusian Princess. One of her parents four princesses. Oh and there was one uncle too.

My mom was their step-sister.

My dad, a dethroned King. Devoid of family, friends and fortune. I guess my mom took pity on him, so here I am.

Try that on for size.

Mr. Rodney Paul Williams
a.k.a
Rodney Paul Banks